# TO TEND AND WATCH OVER

Future Chron Universe

Volume 4

From The Earth Series

Book 4

D.W. PATTERSON

*Seventeenth Printing – May, 2023*

# 1

Davide had often played on the apartment's balcony as a child. After his parents died he had come to the apartment to live with his grandmother. The balcony was the only outdoor play area he had known. Ten by twenty feet, it was huge in comparison to the other apartment balconies. Most had only a fourth of the area. Davide inherited the apartment when his grandmother died and he knew she had inherited it from her grandmother. Davide thought it may have always been in the family.

Davide was short with large hands that gently did his bidding. He made enough money by contracting out the robots inherited from his family that he didn't need to work, at least not full time. Sometimes he would do some illustrations for extra money. Sometimes he would write a story and put it up for sale on a website. He was quite creative in that way.

All this activity was done over the net. He never invited anyone into his apartment and he never went out unless it was absolutely necessary.

He did have one companion, a robotic server that his grandmother had left him. Davide called the robot Sigmund because of his penchant to ask Davide how he felt each morning. Probably a trait impressed upon him by grandmother, thought Davide.

Sigmund wasn't the latest in Artificial Intelligence, he was an early ANI (Artificial Narrow Intelligence) model. He could learn through repeated experience but couldn't change his programming to optimize that learning, as would be true of Artificial General Intelligence if ever it appeared. An ANI in a personal assistant device was called an Annie. Artificial General Intelligence was what most people thought of as AI if they thought about it at all.

Though Sigmund could be upgraded to add capabilities, Davide couldn't afford it, and anyway, Sigmund was capable of handling all the contract robots and the house bots used for cleaning and doing minor maintenance around the apartment. Sigmund, after watching Davide and Davide's grandmother for years, could cook a bit as well. But Davide usually found the resulting meals somewhat lacking in their flavor profile.

Davide's apartment was in one of the complex's towers. These towers were the logical consequence of the skyscrapers of an earlier era. The complex of towers served the needs of land conservation and energy conservation well enough, they were bright and shiny in their own way, but most people still tried to personalize their apartments, they tried to make them their own even if many were government issue.

People in government-issue apartments usually had no robots to contract out, they had no skills to sell that could not be done just as well by a robot. They found that relying on the government was not a reliable answer to their problems when administrations changed. But most had no alternative.

For its part, the government felt that the towers were an expedient way to organize and provide for the masses. Masses that couldn't be expected to provide for themselves.

Davide knew from the net that somewhere there were no towers. There were no crowded billions living in artificially lighted apartments where two rooms were the standard for one person or four. Only Davide and large composite families had more than two rooms.

Davide knew, but had not personally seen, the open spaces beyond the tower complexes. Websites had shown him pictures. Some sites said there was more open land now than when his grandmother was a child. That made sense to Davide because other sites told him that the population of the Earth had stopped growing and had stabilized in the middle of the twenty-first century. Many websites said it had actually diminished, contradicting official government statistics. Davide had thought about applying for immigration to one of the open spaces but though the government didn't prohibit such immigration it was a slow process. In fact, the only instance he knew of where such immigration was approved had taken years to process.

He could imagine the wide-open spaces, he liked to do so while sitting on his balcony in the sun. There was enough sunlight on the balcony to do something that he thought would have made his grandmother proud.

# 2

Davide noticed the delivery drone as it left the package on his balcony.

He fetched the package and excitedly opened it to find a box with the seeds he had ordered online. Davide took the packet of seeds out of the box and set them on his kitchen table. He carefully opened the packet and spread the seeds on a moist paper towel. He was almost shaking with emotion. He remembered doing this with his grandmother when he was a child. He picked up the first planter.

Sigmund interrupted his reverie. "Davide may I ask you what you have there?"

"These are tomato seeds Sigmund."

"Really! What are we going to do with them?"

Davide hesitated, "Sigmund, you know how much I appreciate you. But this is a little project that I had planned for myself."

"Ah, I see," said Sigmund, seemingly deflated. "You would rather I didn't help you with your project then?"

"Not at the beginning, maybe later, okay?"

"Of course Davide, my only purpose is to help you, but I understand, if you would excuse me I have some chores." Sigmund shuffled off into the other room trailed by the vacuum bot.

*Sigmund can be prickly sometimes, I wonder where he got it?*

Davide assembled everything necessary to plant the seeds. He picked up the first planter and prepared it with potting soil and growth formula. He didn't notice Sigmund peeking through the open bedroom door.

He began planting by carefully pressing the tomato seeds into the soil. He continued planting the seeds until he had all thirty-six planters sown. He then placed all the planters on trays and set the trays on a table in his bedroom under growing lamps.

Davide was careful to keep the temperature in the apartment between seventy and eighty degrees. Day after day when he awoke Davide anxiously checked the plants for signs of germination. One morning he found the slightest of seedlings curling out of the soil. Davide immediately moved the seedling to the table he had set up in front of the balcony doors. There the plants could get sufficient light if turned regularly.

He caught Sigmund investigating the seedlings one morning, Davide cautioned him not to touch.

In the next few days, twenty-two of the plants had germinated and Davide had placed them on the sunlit table. It soon became apparent that not all the seeds would germinate. He looked at the barren planters which contained seeds that didn't germinate. He felt he couldn't just dump them down the garbage chute. That seemed a harsh way to dispose of a failed life. Instead, he emptied the planters carefully into the garden plot he had prepared on the balcony.

For several weeks Davide turned the plants several times a day. He relished the opportunity, the chance to care for a living thing. In a few weeks, he was transplanting the tomatoes into larger planters when he noticed a slight yellowing on one side of the leaves of several of the plants. Davide became anxious. He immediately checked his Annie device to see if he could diagnose the condition.

By using the camera in his Annie he searched for matching images. The device matched his pictures with a fungus called *Fusarium* wilt.

The fungi that caused the wilt entered through the roots and spread throughout the water-conducting vessels.

The only strategy to control the spread of the fungus was to destroy the affected plants. The Annie also suggested that the other plants should be replanted in new soil as a precaution. Davide quickly went through the plants looking for the yellowing. He gathered all the plants with symptoms and placed them in a plastic container. He immediately sealed and took the container to the garbage disposal.

Davide began replanting immediately. When he was finished with the planters he called for Sigmund and explained that he needed his help to dig up the outside area and place the old soil in plastic containers. All these containers he and Sigmund hauled to the garbage disposal. They finished late the next morning. Davide was tired and emotionally exhausted, Sigmund needed a recharge. Davide went to bed hoping that he had caught the disease in time to save the rest of the plants.

He dreamed of his grandmother and her tomato garden. In the dream, he was trying to warn her about the fungus but she couldn't hear him. He began yelling at her but still no response. He felt himself falling and woke with a cry.

He lay in bed without sleeping until dusk when he finally slept fitfully.

Davide's anxiety lasted for several days. The only way he could find relief was by inspecting each of the tomato plants for yellowing leaves. It wasn't until a week after the replanting that he started to relax as all the remaining plants seemed to be healthy and growing quickly.

Another few weeks and it was time to replant the tomatoes in the plant box on the balcony where they would finish maturing and bear fruit. This he allowed Sigmund to help with. Sigmund asked many questions as they worked. It reminded Davide of him and his grandmother.

"Why do you ask so many questions Sigmund?" asked Davide.

"It's my programming Davide. It compels me to ask. Do you have such programming?"

"I think I know what you mean. Sometimes I feel compelled to do things too, like raising these tomatoes."

They finished by replanting the flowers that had been saved when the box's soil was replaced. The flowers were planted amongst the tomato plants.

# 3

Sofia Moretti had lived with her grandmother now for six months. After the death of her parents, she and her siblings had been split up. The younger children were dispersed among the remaining aunts and uncles. Sofia being the oldest, it was decided that she could live with her grandmother and take care of her.

They lived in a typical two-room apartment with a separate bath. Sofia's grandmother slept in the second room because she needed a comfortable bed. Sofia made up her bed each night on the couch in the common room which served as the living area and kitchen. Sofia's grandmother had a few house bots but no supervisory robot, so Sofia took on that role.

Sofia was just folding her bedding when her grandmother came into the room. "Good morning grandmother," said Sofia.

"Ah Sofia, why have you not made my coffee? You know the machine does a poor job, I really prefer that you make it."

Sofia knew what was coming next. The lecture. She had heard it so many times she could recite it by heart. Grandmother was very predictable. "I'm sorry grandmother but I have just awoken myself."

"Child when I was your age I was already up and out the door. I would have been at work by now. You don't seem to realize how easy you have it. I hope the Ems can continue making this system work, if not for my sake, then for the sake of you young people who don't seem to be able to take care of yourselves."

The Ems again thought Sofia.

No doubt that the Emulated brains, copies of human brains running in computers, had brought order to chaos. But at the cost of the serendipity that used to make life and invention worthwhile.

"You don't remember before the Ems," said her grandmother. "We all had to work just to stay alive. Men, women and children. I think that from the time the first Ems appeared until I and most other people were able to retire in leisure was less than a decade. They say more invention happened in that decade than in the previous thousand years. And I believe it."

"Grandmother, I know the history of the Ems. I assure you I do appreciate the medical advances, the human life extension, the brain restoration capabilities and I have many friends that swear by their group mind experiences."

"But the price for that is complete subservience to these minds, which however much we may appreciate them, have their own agenda for society which may or may not be the same as ours."

"Not the same as ours!" exclaimed her grandmother. "You mean living in safety and security is not our agenda? Because that is what the Ems have provided. Honestly, I think we need the old schools back where they would teach you young people the real history of the past. Now we have all these network certifiers, obviously, they aren't doing the job when it comes to recent history."

Her grandmother shook her head and mumbled as she headed for the kitchen to make her coffee.

Funny, thought Sofia, grandmother will defend the Ems against any criticism but doesn't trust an automatic coffee maker. It's logic like that which has kept us from controlling our own destinies these past years. I'm so glad I have somewhere to go, I'm so glad I met Arlo.

# 4

Arlo had discovered the field when quite young. He remembered that as a boy he had always liked to explore the complex. His mom had given him a map and on it, he marked off each tower he had visited. By the age of twelve, he had worked through all four quarters. There was only one area that he had not explored to his satisfaction, the core.

But that area was off-limits, to humans anyway. The Ems had taken up residence there when they had contracted with the complex's government to manage the complex. Arlo had heard that the Ems needed to be tightly packed to perform their duties, at the speed they operated minimizing communication times between Ems was critical for efficiency. It was said that there was no room for humans in the Em area and that only specialized robots could make their way in the kilometers and kilometers of cables and equipment so as to maintain the hardware the emulations ran on. But twelve-year-old Arlo didn't believe it.

He would have to plan his "assault" on the Em area carefully. From his tower, it would take a couple of hours to walk there. His friend Pauli would go with him.

Arlo and Pauli researched the history of the complex. They came up with a plan to break into the Em core.

Setting out early one morning they arrived at the core before noon. Around the square that made up the Em core were three old skyscrapers left over from the city era. These had been the tallest buildings of their time. To make them even taller they had been reinforced with an exoskeleton and upper floors had been added. Faster high-speed elevators and new stairs had been added at the same time but if what Arlo and Pauli thought was true, inside at least one of the old buildings would be an intact stairwell from the original design. It would provide emergency access to the city's old subway system and that stairwell would lead them to the core.

"There it is," said Pauli. As they approached the first old building.

"Okay, let's go," said Arlo.

They went into the building and to the location where they expected to find the old elevators. Looking around the area they could find no elevators and no entrance to a stairwell.

"Let's go," said Arlo. "The next building is just a couple of blocks south."

As before they went to the area off the lobby where they expected the old elevators would have been located. The old elevators were still there and they were operational.

"This is it," said Pauli too loudly.

"Shhh, quiet," said Arlo. "We don't want to attract attention."

Pauli's face reddened a bit.

As before they looked around the elevator area for a stairwell entrance but found nothing.

They searched the third building also without luck.

Back on the street Pauli said, "I don't understand it. According to our research, we should have found the stairwell in one of those buildings."

"I know," said Arlo. "Let's take a break and get some lunch, maybe we missed something."

They stopped at a deli to get a sandwich and think about what they should do next.

"Okay," said Arlo. "Assuming our research and conclusion were correct, we missed something."

"How do we know our conclusion is correct?"

"Well if it isn't it doesn't matter right now. We can review the research when we get back home. But right now I don't want to give up."

Pauli shook his head in agreement. They both ate silently for a few minutes.

Arlo stopped eating suddenly. "I've got an idea, come on."

Pauli hurried after Arlo, trying to run and finish his sandwich at the same time.

They arrived back at the second old building, the one with the elevators intact.

Rushing inside and up to the elevators, Arlo punched the up button. He was holding the door open as Pauli slid to a stop.

"Come on," said Arlo, "I've got an idea."

At first, Arlo was unsure about which floor to chose but finally decided on the second. He figured he might as well start his search on the lowest floor and hope.

Getting off on the second floor they walked around the elevator core to the backside and found nothing.

"What is it?" asked Pauli. "What are we doing?"

"Come on," said Arlo. "Let's try the third floor."

It wasn't until the fourth floor that Arlo found what he was looking for, a door marked 'Maintenance – Do Not Enter'. It was locked. But that wouldn't be a problem. As Pauli watched for building occupants Arlo set his Annie to work. The Annie quickly linked to the lock's wireless and began a code-breaking assault. Arlo had trained the Annie on his virtual reality system at home for this eventuality. After a few minutes, click-pop. The Annie had deciphered the key, the door was open.

Was it possible that no one had tried the door before? Maybe, thought Arlo, as most people did not have the same adventurous spirit. So it was quite possible he and Pauli were the first.

They pushed the door further open, it was the stairwell. The way up was blocked but the way down was open. Arlo started to get excited as he descended.

"This is it Pauli. We've found the way in, I know it."

After walking down several flights without finding another way out they emerged through the only available door onto a platform.

"Just as we thought," said Pauli. "The old subway."

The old subway was no longer used but was maintained for purposes other than those for which it was originally designed. They heard a rumble in the distance and moved back into the shadows. It was a two-car train, obviously automated. It came from the direction of the complex's periphery and it was headed into the core. Arlo was sure.

He jumped off the platform.

"Come on Pauli," he turned back to say. "We go in the direction of the train. Be careful, remember that third rail is electrified."

Jumping down to the roadbed Pauli started running after Arlo in the direction the train was taking. It wasn't long until they came upon a gate across the tracks. Apparently it activated automatically when a train approached. They would have to wait.

Within half an hour the gate started to slide back, both of them scurried through as they heard a train approaching. They hid in the shadows against the tunnel wall until the train had passed. The gate closed. They were in the Em core.

# 5

There were regulations about homegrown food but at the time Davide was growing his tomatoes he didn't know about them. Although it wasn't strictly against the law to plant a vegetable garden, government regulations made it almost impossible for the average citizen to do so. The certifications and credentials required to legally grow vegetables cost a lot of money. They usually were sought after only by corporations and professionals working for corporations.

Most people relied on the grocery stores in their towers for fruits and vegetables. There they could get government-certified organics or bio-engineered foods. But the cost of certification made the organics expensive. Prohibited from growing their own and finding the price of organics too high most people bought and ate the cheaper engineered foods.

The government used automated drones to enforce domestic regulations such as the one for homegrown food. Through a public relations campaign, the government tried to convince the people that the drones were for their safety but the inhabitants of the towers knew the drones were really there to prevent them from committing regulatory offenses. The drones very effectively dissuaded the majority of citizens from pursuing projects that could have made them more self-reliant.

Davide hadn't paid much attention to the drones. Or at least he had trusted they were there for his welfare. They were quiet and unobtrusive most of the time. But they had been watching Davide's balcony ever since he had ordered the seeds from the online website. Davide knew nothing of this until the door chimed and there was a knock.

His Annie showed the door viewer where Davide saw a couple of people and several robots, one man was showing his ID to the viewer. It was building maintenance. Davide opened the door and immediately was pushed out of the way by the robots. The two men took Davide aside and began to question him.

"You are Davide Ephraim Jackson?" asked one of the men, the tallest.

"Yes," said Davide.

"You live here in this apartment alone?"

"Yes, except for my robot."

"Mr. Jackson did you know it was against government regulations to grow vegetables without being a certified grower?"

"No, I'm sorry, I did not. I thought it was no different than flowers."

"Mr. Jackson, do you realize the damage you could do to yourself and to others if you distributed such items?"

"No sir, I guess not."

"That's the problem Mr. Jackson, so many people are unaware of the danger such plants pose to the public at large. We understand that you had a problem with a particular fungus. Is that so?"

"Yes I did, but I've completely removed it from my garden, how did you know?" asked Davide as he turned to look at his garden. He almost shouted when he saw the robots digging up his garden plot and placing it into plastic bags. "What are they doing?" he demanded. "They can't do that!"

Davide's yell brought Sigmund out of the other room but he froze when he saw all the robots on the balcony.

"Yes Mr. Jackson they can. Here is the seizure warrant, it is all legal." He handed Davide the paper and continued.

"As I was saying, you and others don't understand the damage to the food supply you could cause by these unlicensed home vegetable gardens. Without the proper training and inspection, such diseases as the fungus that attacked your plants could spread. A disruption in the food supply is a very serious matter. You wouldn't want to be responsible for such an incident would you?"

"No of course not. I just wanted to grow a few plants as I remembered my grandmother doing."

"I understand Mr. Jackson," said the man in a consoling tone. "It is a common mistake. Still, it is a violation of current regulations and you will have to take the punishment. Of course, you may be represented by an attorney if you wish. But I would recommend you accept the judge's verdict and get on with your life. Court cases can take months to schedule and conclude. And the juried verdicts are usually the same as when uncontested."

Davide's eyes were near to tears as he watched the last of his plants being pulled up and placed in the hazmat bags. He no longer was angry but felt only a sad resignation. "I'll do whatever you say sir," he said quietly.

# 6

The new apartment was dark. Two rooms and a small bath. The larger room was a kitchen/living room combination. The bedroom was eight by ten. It was on a lower floor with only a small balcony, barely large enough to stand on. Davide had been here a month and had only seen a sliver of sunlight during high noon. It was the judge's decision that he move from his grandmother's apartment. It was okay though, he could afford it and the apartment matched his mood.

Sigmund had spent the past day learning the new apartment's arrangement so that he could do his chores and direct the few house bots that came with the apartment. Davide had heard him talking to himself. Davide knew that Sigmund was just trying to speed his learning by repeating to himself but in Davide's present state of mind it made Sigmund seem as lost and confused as Davide himself felt. Even though he didn't ask, Davide reassured Sigmund several times that it was not his fault that they had ended up here. The door buzzed.

There was no viewer so Davide looked through the peephole. He couldn't see anyone. He opened the door slightly and saw a package. Retrieving the package he saw that it was from a website with a name similar to the one that he had ordered the tomato seeds from. He was alarmed.

*Why are they sending me something, what if someone finds out, where will I end up next?*

Davide hid the package in his closet, telling Sigmund not to touch it, trying to forget about it.

Several days later when there hadn't been any more knocks on the door Davide sat down in the closet doorway and took out the package. He opened it slowly and found an object in a brown paper wrapper. Removing the wrapper paper Davide found a slim book, a book about growing tomatoes. His eyes watered but he put the book away.

As time went on Davide and Sigmund became familiar with their new lives, Sigmund even stopped talking to himself. The book had sat on the wall shelf in Davide's bedroom all this time without being opened. It was late at night as he was struggling to sleep that Davide took the book down from the shelf. He opened it to find a picture of a fully formed mature tomato plant gracing the title page. The copyright page had an old date but the book seemed newly printed.

Davide spent the rest of the night reading and looking at the pictures in the book. Especially the pictures of plants in the sunshine. Each picture in the sunshine stirred memories. It wasn't long until he could hear his grandmother's voice in his head. She loved to talk to him as they worked in the balcony garden.

He remembered using a short stick to create a shallow hole in the soil. She would follow him, dropping seeds and tamping the soil. She would tell him stories about her childhood and about the childhoods of her mother and grandmother. Davide remembered a story she had told him about past relatives.

A story about people living, not in the towers, but on the land in a small house. The story claimed that these people grew a lot of their own food. Grandmother said she didn't know if the story was true or not, it had been passed down through so many. But she thought it was true. She thought it was a lovely idea anyway. And so did Davide.

Davide closed the book. He needed to get outside. The balcony was lit in the glow of the lights from the surrounding towers. It wasn't satisfying. He needed to get outside.

# 7

It had been more than a decade (human subjective time) since the Em had taken the job offered by the complex's government. The job had paid enough to allow the Em to grow his family and provide job security for them. The Em was very much a family man.

The contract had called for a test installation before widespread deployment. The Em and the government agreed upon a centrally located area for the Ems to occupy. Several towers were turned over to them. The Em relocated to one of them and immediately started having the infrastructure installed that would be needed to support a large nest of Ems.

When resources allowed, the Em imprinted or reanimated another member of his "family". The Em called it "budding". In each family, all new Ems were of the same imprinted brain but those reanimated also had their experiences since first budding restored. Each was given a particular area of the complex's infrastructure to tend and watch over. As more and more Ems came online the complex's residents begin to notice the changes.

Transportation was the first area the Ems had transformed. They quickly reduced the commute time, at least for those that still commuted, to only a few minutes across the whole of the complex. The food got fresher, at least for those who could afford real food. The high belt traffic, mostly delivery drone traffic that operated at the highest levels of the towers, became more orderly, quicker, and quieter because the Ems had redesigned it.

Crime, something that threatened the very concept of the complexes, came under control. By increasing their processor speed and assigning more Em buds, the Ems had been able to monitor all the complex's camera installations and drone feedback in real-time, something the complex's government had never been able to do. They could then respond with their robot surrogates in cooperation with the human police to stop the crime.

The Ems infrastructure continued to grow. They built their towers higher and higher until the Em core overshadowed the rest of the complex. When the communication delays up and down the towers became prohibitive, the Ems requested more structures on the core's periphery.

Displaced residents complained but overall the complex's other residents felt that the results of Em management outweighed the sacrifices made by a few.

The test installation became permanent when the time came for contract renewal because it was apparent to the complex's government that they could no longer operate without Em management. The government didn't even complain when the price of the new contract went up, after all, the Ems were saving the government enough on operating expenses to cover the contract cost.

But there were a few residents of the complex that weren't completely satisfied with the new situation. Particularly with the real-time surveillance which they felt could be abused by the Ems and the government. These residents spent time and money making sure that their apartments weren't monitored and that they could not be followed using their Annies or other electronic devices. Some even went to the trouble of escaping the complex or at least knowing how to escape if it became necessary.

# 8

Standing in the open field Arlo was remembering when he was twelve years old. He and his best friend Pauli had made it into the Em core.

After passing through the gate across the subway rails they found the lighting in the core to be very dim. But not the noise. The racket was intense but the source was far off.

After their eyes adjusted to the dim lighting they wandered toward the noise. They soon found themselves in a large area with multiple tracks and wide platforms.

"This must have been a large train station," said Arlo to Pauli. Pauli nodded.

Arlo pointed at the double doors on the platform. "I think the noise is coming from in there, come on."

Carefully pushing one of the doors open enough for them to slip through they found rows and rows of pumps and turbines. Moving closer to the pumps Arlo put his hand near the piping of one and felt an intense cold. He jerked his hand away.

"What's wrong are you hurt?"

"No," said Arlo. "It's just cold."

Arlo looked up and saw that the piping disappeared above him. It went through the ceiling and was covered in frost with icicles hanging down. He said to Pauli, "The pipes must be for the cooling of the computer equipment running the emulations."

They were so deafened by the noise around them that they almost revealed themselves to the robots crossing the far end of the room.

Pauli grabbed Arlo's shoulder when he saw the robots and pulled him down behind a pump. He pointed to the robots.

The robots were pushing equipment carts laden with what appeared to be electronic equipment. They were loading a large freight elevator. Once the elevator was packed the robots sent it on its way and turned to push their carts back the way they came.

When the robots disappeared around the corner Arlo and Pauli ran over to the elevator. They hesitated a moment.

Pauli said, "Should we take the elevator or use the stairs, if stairs exist?"

"Let's look for the stairs," said Arlo. "I don't want to get trapped in some elevator."

After a short search, they found the stairs around the corner. They started up.

Arlo pushed the first door he came to slightly open. He felt a rush of warm air and heard the sound of fans somewhere. After a time, not seeing or hearing any movement, he was confident enough to push the door further open and walk into the room. Looking around he saw equipment stacked to the ceiling and beyond, for the ceiling had been completely cut up to accommodate all the stacks and piping.

Arlo motioned for Pauli to follow him.

Arlo looked up, the stack of equipment seemed to go on for at least forty or fifty feet, even through other ceilings. Each piece of equipment was encased in what looked to Arlo like a plastic. It gave off multicolored lights, pulsing sometimes in unison, sometimes randomly. With the low overall lighting, the effect was somewhat eerie.

Each stack was configured in a hexagonal circle with piping running through the center. From the central piping smaller pipes, like vesicles, extended into the plastic substance. Arlo was looking at the physical manifestation of thousands of Ems in one room, other rooms contained similar installations.

He was just about to walk around the cluster when he heard a voice.

"You two shouldn't be here," said a man's voice.

Arlo spun around to see a man dressed in a white smock. "I, I was just curious," said Arlo. Pauli nodded.

"We know about you two, especially you Arlo, we've known about your "curiosity" for some time. May I show you boys around?"

Arlo was a bit stunned. "Yes please," he said quietly.

The man lead Arlo and Pauli around the periphery of the room. He said, "And what you see here are the fast Ems. Being closer to the cooling system they can run their hardware faster than other Ems higher up because the processor cooling is at maximum in this room. These Ems are typically running a million times faster than the ones at the top and are running problem-solving simulations which if involving time can be run at about one-hundred years of simulated time in an hour of real-time. Communications with other Ems on this level allow even vaster simulations.

"The Ems farther up in this building are running slower and working on less computationally intensive problems until you get to the top where the emulated brains run only slightly faster than human equivalents. Those Ems are useful for interfacing with humanity as you might expect.

"The equipment you see is encased in a clear material specially designed by the Ems for efficient heat conduction. You may touch the material if you wish," said the man to Pauli.

Pauli looked from the man to the encasing material. With a somewhat worried expression, he slowly reached out to touch the material. The material felt cool to the touch and somewhat nebulous, like touching a thick cloud. Pauli pushed a little harder and the tip of his finger disappeared into the material, almost as if it had been severed.

Pauli let out a yelp and pulled his finger quickly back to find it still in one piece.

The man laughed and said, "It is a trick of light, the refraction index of the material causes what you saw."

He continued, "Besides convection cooling, the pipes carry a cooling substance unlike any known to man which transports the heat away. I believe you saw the pumps and generators that maintain the cooling system in the basement?"

"Yes," Arlo said, quite fascinated.

The rest of the tour proceeded without incident.

When finished the man took Arlo and Pauli down to the basement to wait for a train to take them back. A robot walked up to the pair.

"This is one of the latest Em robots," said the man. "Unlike the robots you are used to this one is quite autonomous and could operate anywhere in the complex without oversight. It is designed by the Ems and is a much more general artificial intelligence."

The robot reached out its "hand" to shake with Arlo.

"Hello," said the robot.

Arlo reached out to shake its hand. Almost immediately he jerked his hand back and rubbed it. Something had pierced the skin of his hand like a needle.

The man spoke up, “Don't worry Arlo. That is a tracking device, smaller than a pinpoint. It won't cause you any problems, it is hypoallergenic and you will quickly forget it. But as I hope you can understand we need some way to track you in case you decide to visit us again.”

Arlo looked from the man to his hand, rubbing his palm. The man helped them into the automated train car and he was gone.

# 9

People walked everywhere now. Even long distances across the complex. There were taxis for people that had difficulties walking. But most were encouraged to walk. The Ems had made it easier to walk by managing the traffic in real-time and favoring pedestrians. And because more people walked, fewer drove or were driven, the overall health of the complex's residents had improved, just as the Ems had planned.

After putting away the book Davide left the apartment and was walking in the direction that would allow him to watch the sunrise at the complex's edge wall. It was still dark when he arrived. The safety wall was in front of him. Beyond was the open space but no one went beyond the safety wall. He was tired but there was nowhere to sit so he sat with his back against the cement wall. He tilted his head back and saw, through the haze of the artificial lighting, a few bright stars. He watched the sky as the first tinge of sunrise shown red above the wall's top. The red tinge brightened faster than he expected until it had overpowered the street and building lights. The streetlights began to shut off. The dark blue of the sky appeared to soften into azure.

The day had begun though it was still relatively quiet here at the edge of the complex. Very few people had business out this way. Many worked at home. Virtual games kept many others occupied. Most people would send a robot out when they needed something or have it delivered by drone. Another behavior modification the Ems had planned to help prevent the spread of disease.

Davide watched the sky brighten and felt his mood lift. He yawned, then got up to go home and sleep.

He awoke in the afternoon. Eating a bite while facing the balcony window, he remembered the sunshine in the pictures of his book. For some reason, those simple photos were more realistic than any of the images he saw on his Annie. He wondered if there were other books with similar pictures.

It wasn't easy searching the net for paper books since everything was published electronically now. His Annie finally found a site that offered some old paper books. He found a gardening book that looked promising and ordered it. It was surprisingly inexpensive for such an object.

He looked at the balcony, it was getting late. He needed to go out. He dressed and told Sigmund he would be back in a couple of hours, he quickly glanced at the book on the shelf as he was leaving. The pleasing thought came to him that soon it would have a companion. He bought some fruit at the grocer downstairs and headed for the complex's edge.

He mostly passed robots on the street running errands or doing work for the Ems or the government. The streetlights had still not come on by the time he arrived at the wall. Again there wasn't anyone nearby or rather there was someone a couple of streets over. The slight curve of the wall almost hid them but there was definitely someone there.

Davide didn't let the discovery bother him. He sat down as he had done that morning with his back to the wall and his head turned upward. Between peeks at the sky, he took some of his fruit out to eat. The apple wasn't entirely ripe although the red peel made it look so. Like everything else he bought in the stores that was inexpensive, there was something not quite right about the merchandise. Still, it was good enough.

The sky above him was becoming golden as he watched. He didn't even notice the girl approach.

"Hi," she said. "I haven't seen you here before."

"Oh hello," said Davide. "I'm new here." The girl was thin and tall, probably his age thought Davide. Her eyes were large with a touch of mischief.

"My name is Sofia."

"I am Davide."

"I come here quite often. It gets me out of the small apartment I share with my grandmother, it also gets me out of bad moods."

"I know what you mean. I have some fruit here if you would like." Sofia thanked him and took an apple from the bag.

"I should bring a snack like this when I come here." Sofia continued talking while Davide listened. He was a little concerned about revealing too much to a stranger.

They sat silently the last few minutes watching the sky become a deep yellow-orange and then the streetlights came on. "Well," said Sofia. "That's it for today, maybe I'll see you here again?"

"Sure," said Davide. He watched her round the tower corner before he got up to go home.

# 10

The Em had found most humans easy enough to handle. It was easy to give them what they thought they wanted while at the same time giving them what they really needed. The Em had found only one exception to this rule, a person known only to the Em as Jaj.

This person had completely frustrated the Em's efforts to find out who and where he was. The Em suspected that because of the slight communications delay he detected Jaj was off-planet, but the Em couldn't be sure because every trace that the Em ran was blocked. The Em was baffled for the first time since his imprinting.

Because he could maintain his anonymity Jaj caused the Em some worry even though at other times the Em sought Jaj's advice.

This was one of those times.

"It seems," said the Em. "That we have a few people who are not adapting well to the new situation they find themselves in. As a matter of fact, we've had this problem since we began."

"There are always a few," said Jaj.

"Yes but if I may ask. How would you handle these exceptions?"

"It is always best with humans to allow them to feel a certain amount of self-determination."

"What do you mean exactly?"

"Some people need to feel that they control the decisions they make. They will push back against any effort to direct their lives."

"I see," said the Em. "It is strange to me that even though I was imprinted from a human brain, I don't seem to have such a desire. I wonder if this compulsion for control is intellectual at all. Maybe some animal instinct that can't be imprinted."

"Maybe, I don't really know. Maybe the lack of sensorial input?"

"We have experimented with such," said the Em. "But except for the need to expand our multitasking capability, it hasn't led to any emergent property. And all the human writings on the subject only end up in a kind of metaphysical miasma."

"Well if the Ems haven't figured it out then I'm sure I have nothing to add. But getting back to your earlier question what I would suggest you do is give them a little room. Room to feel that they have some control over their lives, that it is not all planned for them by some brain in a box, no offense."

"None taken," said the Em. "What you say can be done. Of course, they will need to be kept under surveillance but that shouldn't be too hard. And if they become a disturbing element . . ."

"Excuse me. If you will allow me I can help you with their management. After all who could be better qualified than one of their fellow-creatures?"

"I see what you mean. I will take your offer into consideration. I can see where having a human for consultation might be an advantage in our system."

"Very well then. When you are ready to use my services contact me."

The Em thought for many cycles after finishing the talk with Jaj. It was obviously a good solution to managing these problem elements. But at the same time, it would set a dangerous precedent. That Ems needed humans.

# 11

A few weeks after twelve-year-old Arlo had visited the Em core he had decided to hike the subway in the other direction to see what he could find. Pauli didn't accompany him. In that direction, Arlo found that the subway emerged from its tunnel into the open and that was where he found the field.

The field became Arlo's new playground. He even began camping there. Slowly over time, Arlo had asked others that he knew to join him. Even though it was quite a hike the field became the center of the group's life. The feeling of being away from the constricting rules and regulations of the complex was greater than the effort it took to get there.

Now a decade later Arlo, Pauli and a few others had come out for a day in the field. They had left before daylight and light was just breaking when they emerged onto the field.

It wasn't long until the group had company, a security drone was overhead.

One of the group, Justin, pointed it out. "How do they know when we are here?"

"I suspect the Ems are still able to track me," said Arlo. "Even after ten years, they are my constant companion. But never mind, except for watching they've never done anything to interfere with my activities."

"I agree," said Pauli. "They are not going to bother us unless we do something to upset their management of the complex. I'm afraid that is why we lost a few of our number. They wanted to be too confrontational. I hope we all realize that this is not the time or place for such, we are too weak and they are too strong."

"That's right," said one of the girls, Rosalyn. "And I have no interest in confrontation, so if the group is into that, then I'm out."

The others agreed.

Arlo had so far been able to organize the group through his personality and charisma. But he knew they needed something more, something to coalesce around. He had decided that self-sufficiency, as far as was possible, would be the group's goal. And self-sufficiency started with food and shelter.

The group put up some temporary shelter in the form of tents. They worked to build a cistern to capture the rain. This was easily purified for use. They even got a rudimentary waste disposal system working by using some modified technology from the government's abandoned space program.

Soon they had an area where they could go and spend a day and night, maybe longer if they brought enough food. But that was the problem, backpacking enough food for an extended stay was an effort. They were soon trying to grow food on-site. The attempt was not a complete failure but it wasn't a success either. Growing food meant tending the fields every day and that meant a long hike there and back even if staying overnight.

Someone with experience and drive was needed to get the growing to the scale needed to provision the group. Everyone kept alert to the possibility of attracting such a person to fill the need.

# 12

The door buzzed and Davide went to look through the peephole he'd recently installed. No one was there so he opened the door slightly and looked down, it was a package. It was from the gardening book's website. Davide placed the package on the kitchen table and proceeded to open it. He took out the large gardening book. Sigmund joined him.

Davide opened the book and saw that on each page were beautiful color pictures of garden vegetables. Planting and harvesting information was also available for each plant. Growing seasons were given.

Even Sigmund seemed impressed, except for the tomatoes he and Davide had grown, he had never seen vegetables in the field. Davide listened to Sigmund's comments but the pictures of the sunshine glued his eyes to the page.

The day went by without notice until the dimming light announced the arrival of evening. Davide, now alone as Sigmund did chores, closed the book and quickly dressed, he yelled to Sigmund that he was going out. He hurried downstairs to buy his fruit and head for the wall of the complex. He arrived in plenty of time to watch the onset of dusk.

He looked up the curve of the wall to where he first saw Sofia but no one was there. He was disappointed but soon became engrossed in the last display of the setting sun.

It wasn't until he could count the stars on both hands that he got up to go home.

Each morning and evening when he went to the complex's edge he glanced down the curve of the wall and saw no one. It was the fourth day and she hadn't shown up again. Oh well, he told himself, it had been a chance meeting, to begin with so he shouldn't expect anything more.

One morning after his vigil, Davide stopped to do some shopping. After shopping he was almost back to his tower when he heard a voice behind him, he turned and there was Sofia with a large carry-all slung over her shoulder. "Ah, Sofia," he said. "I haven't seen you for a few days."

"Hi Davide," she said. "I know I've been busy at home."

"Sure I understand."

"Is this your building?"

"Yes it is," said Davide trying to think of something else to say. "Sofia I was wondering if you would like to come up and see the collection of gardening books I have."

"Books, you mean paper books? No one has those anymore."

"Well I have a couple."

"Oh," she said. Sofia wasn't worried about Davide, she could handle herself well enough in such circumstances but she was in a hurry, still, she was intrigued by the fact he bought gardening books. "I guess I have a few minutes, maybe I could use your bathroom while I'm there?"

"Sure," said Davide.

They were both quiet on the short elevator ride to Davide's floor.

"Here we are," said Davide as they entered his apartment. "It's just two rooms, not much really."

"No, it's nice."

"Well, here is the living room as you can see, and over there is the bedroom." Sofia quickly looked around and walked over to the bedroom door, glancing inside, she saw Sigmund.

"Hello," she said.

Sigmund responded. Davide then introduced Sofia to Sigmund and Sigmund excused himself to work in the kitchen area.

"Oh, look," she said. "Those are the books you told me about on the bookshelf."

"Yes, not much of a library I'm afraid. But do have a look, and there is the bathroom also."

"Thank you. I'll just be a moment," she said as she closed the bedroom door.

Davide sat at his kitchen table waiting. Sigmund asked Davide if Sofia would be staying and should he fix something to eat. Davide said he didn't know. Sigmund was put off.

"Davide," he said. "I simply must know these things ahead of time so that I may properly prepare for your guests."

Davide tried to explain that this wasn't a planned visit and he didn't think Sofia would stay long enough to eat. This seemed to mollify Sigmund as he went back to his chores.

Sofia exited the bedroom and asked, "Have you ever gardened?"

"With my grandmother," Davide said, not wishing to discuss recent events.

"We could use a gardener."

"What do you mean?"

"Well, I guess it might be best to show you, you want to see?"

"I guess so."

"Sigmund," he said. "It looks like I will be going out for some time." Sigmund watched them leave the apartment, he never approved of such abruptness.

# 13

Davide followed Sofia down to the lobby. In front of the tower, Sofia turned and said, "This way." She headed in the direction of the complex's center. Davide walked by her side not saying much.

After a few minutes, he spoke up, "How far are we going?"

"We are going to the center of the complex."

"But that is a long hike on foot. Why don't we take a cab?"

"It's best this way," said Sofia, "you'll see."

Except for a few comments about passing landmarks not much was said between them. Sofia seemed in a hurry and a little tense. Davide was trusting but becoming a bit anxious at Sofia's silence.

Finally, they arrived at one of the oldest towers in the complex. It was actually a refitted skyscraper, who knew how old. And it was located just outside the Em core. Sofia went in the front door with Davide right behind, she immediately went up to the elevators. She and Davide and a couple of delivery robots got into the elevator. Sofia pressed the fourth-floor button and there she and Davide got off. "Okay," she said. "Now we take the stairs down."

"Stairs, down? We just came from the lobby."

"I know, you'll see." Davide followed Sofia around the elevator core, Sofia's Annie opened a door marked maintenance with a cipher key. Once in the stairwell, they started down.

After a few flights, Davide was surprised and asked, "Where's the lobby door?"

“There isn't one. It was sealed when the building was renovated. The other stairwells go to the lobby but this one is sealed off except on the fourth floor.”

“So where are we going?”

“You'll see, we are almost there.”

Davide lost count but thought they must have descended five or six stories. At the bottom, Sofia opened the only door and they emerged onto a platform with very dim lighting.

Sofia said, “This is the old subway platform. It served as a station stop on the subway system.”

“What do you mean?” asked Davide.

“Years ago there were underground trains that the people used to travel from place to place in the city. They were all abandoned when it was decided to optimize the size of the tower complexes for walking. The building we were just in was the last one that had a means of entry to the subway, I guess to make it easy if anyone ever needed to access the subway system but I don't really know why. Now it's only used to maintain the Em core.”

“The Em core! That is strictly off-limits.”

“Don't worry. We are not going anywhere near the Em core, we are going in the opposite direction. But we will have to watch for the work trains and try not to be seen. Come on I'll show you how we use the subway.”

“We?”

“Yes. Me and a few others. Let's go, if we hurry we can make it in a few hours.” She climbed off the platform onto the old roadbed and began walking briskly. The dim lighting continued into the distance, down the tracks.

“But Sofia, it is already late. How far are we going, will we be back before dark?”

Sofia turned and said, “Come or stay Davide, I’m late and haven’t time to explain everything to you.” Davide hesitated before he began chasing after her.

Sofia wouldn't say much about the destination but talked to Davide about what he knew about gardening, especially about growing vegetables. Davide told her his experience was slight but he had successfully grown tomatoes recently, though he didn't tell her the results of his efforts.

“You grew tomatoes? Are you authorized? Did you know about the regulations?”

“No, I’m not authorized and I didn't know at the time I was growing the tomatoes about the regulations but I stopped once I found out.”

It had been late afternoon when they began to walk and avoiding the work trains only added to the walk's duration. Davide had no idea how far or how long they had been walking and he had forgotten his Annie, but he was getting tired and hungry when suddenly Sofia stopped, adjusted the carry-all and pointed to the far wall. There was a ladder scaling the wall.

“We could go further up the tracks but this is a short cut I've found, we go up now.”

Davide waited for Sofia to gain some height before following. After a minute he heard her grunt as if she were pushing something, then a muffled clang. Davide looked up and could see stars framed by a perfectly round opening. Sofia had pulled her legs through the opening and was standing, peering down at Davide. "Come on," she said.

He climbed the ladder and pulled himself up through the hole. The dim light in the tunnel allowed his eyes to quickly adjust to his new surroundings, although he couldn't really see anything but the stars overhead and a glow on the horizon behind the tree line. "Where are we?" he asked.

"We're outside the complex, a few miles. This used to be part of the old city before the complexes were built, we think it was a park. If you look over that way you can see the glow of the lights from our complex." Davide looked where Sofia pointed and saw the horizon lit behind a line of trees. "The other dimmer lights you see are from other tower complexes."

"Come on there's some people I want you to meet. They've been looking for a gardener type."

"But I told you I'm not a gardener, really," protested Davide.

"Close enough," said Sofia.

# 14

The Em had to agree with Jaj. Control theory was only approximately applicable in this case. Allowing a little "slack" in the system was much preferable to a hard failure. Humans made the system brittle in the Em's estimation, meaning it was subject to failure when the slightest difficulties appeared.

The Em was discussing what could be done with other budded Ems. They were mostly known by numbers.

Bud-fourteen spoke, "How about genetically engineering these problem elements to be more passive and accepting of their environment?"

The Em said, "Genetic engineering is possible but it has been outlawed by humans and for good reason. The history of genetically engineering humans has not been a pleasant one. At first, as the engineering had been mostly confined to curing diseases, the humans had supported such efforts. The more common genetic disorders such as autism, many cancers, cystic fibrosis, Parkinson's, sickle cell as well as others began to fall to the new treatments.

"But the list of genetic diseases proved finite and many genetic engineers turned to improving or enhancing the genome to maintain their research capabilities. The proponents of this approach believed that the best way to "predict the future is to change it".

"But for many humans this led to less than desirable tinkering with the human genome. Some approved of this but many simply thought it misguided.

"The opportunity for genetic discrimination had already been outlawed in most countries by the middle of the twenty-first century and when there were accidental releases of gene-modified organisms and then the later deliberate release of modified pathogens the tide turned against genetic engineering. Research was proscribed worldwide soon after."

Bud number twenty-seven spoke up, "This may have been the proper decision for humans at the time with their limited capabilities. But with the assistance of Em engineering this is no longer true. There is no longer a need for lab experiments and the consequent possibility of accidental release because we can run enough simulations to make a determination without real-world testing. And the deliberate release of a modified pathogen is impossible anywhere we monitor.

"Likewise, the real impediments to genetic engineering; such as the multiple contributing factors to genomic expression, the probabilistic nature of genomic inheritance, the broader environmental factors that contribute to genomic expression, all these can now be handled by the massive computational power that we Ems can bring to the problem."

"That is true," said the Em. "But I have found that such straight forward presentations of the facts to humans is not as influential as a picture or a meme of a genetically engineered monstrosity. We are dealing with emotions not logic when we talk about engineering the human genome."

"I agree," said Bud-fourteen. "So that rules out any genetic engineering to solve the problem."

"So what do you think should be done?" asked Bud twenty-seven.

The Em said, "Well since we can't improve the species I suggest that we manage them using the old human art of persuasion. And this is where a contract with the human Jaj would be valuable."

The other Ems soon agreed that the advantages of working with a human outweighed the disadvantages and Jaj was offered a contract which he accepted.

# 15

Sofia and Davide walked toward the center of the opening. Looking around as he walked it appeared to Davide that they were completely surrounded by trees. The opening was probably three hundred feet across, he couldn't tell for sure in the dark.

As they approached the group Davide could make out about six or seven people. Sofia called to one of the group and that person walked out to meet her.

"Hi Arlo," said Sofia as they hugged.

"Sofia, you're late and who have you brought with you?"

"Arlo, this is Davide. Davide is a gardener."

"Is that so Davide?"

Davide couldn't see in the dark very well though he could tell Arlo was taller than himself. "Well, I have some experience growing tomatoes but as I've tried to tell Sofia I'm no expert."

"Sofia, I wish you had asked me before you brought someone with you, but now that it is done. Davide we would like to start growing some vegetables here. Do you think you could accomplish such a thing?"

"Well, I could try. But there are things I'll need, like tools, fertilizer, seeds, water . . ."

"We can get all those things except maybe the water. But maybe we could use the cistern we've built or build another one just for the garden?"

"Yes, I think so. We only need to water when we first plant, after that the rains should take care of most of the plant's water needs."

"Very good, let's give it a try then?"

Davide hesitated for a moment, everything was moving so fast. "Maybe," he said. "But I have a question. I do not have the education and certifications of a professional gardener. Do you or does anyone here?"

"No."

"Well, you know it is against the law for us to grow vegetables, right?"

"Yes."

"So they will just find out and destroy the plants, I've had it done to me."

Sofia looked at Davide.

"I can assure you Davide, the authorities know everything about what we are doing here. We are under constant surveillance from the drones."

"Then why don't they stop you?"

"Because, they consider us harmless and figure that giving us a little space to rebel in satisfies our needs. They know they can always close in at any time."

"I don't get it. I grow a few tomatoes and I am punished by losing my home. You do much worse and no one cares?"

"Well there you have it, that explains it."

"Explains it?" asked Davide perplexed.

"Yes. You had something that someone wanted. They used the law to take it from you. I bet if you could find out who has your old home you will find someone with connections in the government. Now let's get something to eat."

# 16

What Arlo had said really bothered Davide. Breaking a law you didn't know existed was one thing, but losing your home to someone more politically connected than you was unforgivable. A government that would allow such a thing was not deserving of voluntary compliance. Such a government had only coercion and force left to accomplish its ends. He had decided he would grow the garden after hearing Arlo's explanation of governmental misconduct. It was the first time that Davide had ever knowingly broken a rule.

The months passed and the garden grew. Davide studied the books he had bought and sent away for more. He spent almost every hour of daylight in the open field. He started before dawn and walked back home after dusk. Sigmund prepared his food, maintained the other robots, and the apartment and wondered if he could go with Davide. Davide explained that it was too far for Sigmund's battery power and Davide hadn't the money to upgrade it. Sigmund accepted the explanation but remained concerned about being separated from Davide so much.

As for Davide, he was happy with his new life. He had even forgotten the bitterness he had felt towards the government which had prompted him to start the garden.

The garden itself was a time machine. When Davide was there the hours stopped their march. The years dissolved, his grandmother was beside him again. The plants that took so much care gave back to him their fruit.

His hands had hardened with calluses but still, they could gently manipulate the plants. He could sun under a blue sky or bathe in a summer rain. He was sure this was where he was meant to be, this was what he was meant to do.

The others had helped by bringing out the tools and fertilizer themselves or if they had them, sending supplies out on their smart carts. The carts could roll or walk or climb, whatever was necessary to make their deliveries. Some even rode their smart carts to the field. There were many more people than Davide had first thought. And they were all young, about his age. They helped with the weeding and harvesting which Davide directed.

Some brought newer ANI-based robots that could be taught to garden. Davide thought this a waste, to work with your hands in the dirt and with the plants was a reward, not a chore. But he said nothing.

After he found out that Sofia and Arlo were together he didn't much think about them or the others. His schedule wasn't theirs. He came before anyone and usually left after everyone, unless they were spending the night. Davide never spent the night. This was his vocation, not his avocation. The garden was where he worked, the apartment was where he slept, somehow mixing the two seemed wrong.

Arlo was right about the government, the drones were Davide's constant companions. Obviously, the watchers knew who he was and what he was doing. They could have stopped him at any time but hadn't.

Davide picked a couple of tomatoes and headed home for the day.

# 17

Davide was tired when he got home. He had just set his tomatoes on the kitchen table and greeted Sigmund when the door buzzed. Through the peephole, he could see a couple of men in suits.

Davide opened the door and the closest man said, "Are you Davide Ephraim Jackson?"

"Yes sir," said Davide.

"May we come in?" asked the man.

"Of course."

The men sat on the couch across from Davide. One man was impeccably dressed, the other man's suit was ill-fitting.

"Mr. Jackson, my name is Alberto Alisi", said the well-dressed man. "And this is Ugo Vicenzi. We are here to talk to you about the gardening you've been doing."

"Are you from the government?" asked Davide apprehensively.

"No," said Mr. Alisi with a smile. "Our employer is not associated with the government. But he is interested in what you have been doing out in the field a few miles from here."

Davide turned to Sigmund and said, "Sigmund would you excuse us." Sigmund went into the bedroom but could still hear them.

"How do you know what I've been doing?"

"While our employer is not part of the government he does have some connections that keep him informed of matters that may interest him. And what you have been doing out there in that field is of interest to him.

You might say he has been watching over you ever since your first efforts to grow tomato plants. You no doubt received the book he sent?"

Vicenzi spoke up in a deeply accented Italian that wasn't heard much anymore.

"You might also be interested in knowing that if not for our employer your activities and those of your friends would have attracted the negative attention of the complex's government. I believe you have attracted their attention before?"

"Yes. But at that time I didn't know I was doing anything that should attract their attention."

"But you do now?" asked Alisi.

"Yes."

"Well, we didn't mention the past to embarrass you but just to emphasize the advantages of having our employer as a benefactor."

"Okay," said Davide somewhat confused. "I think I understand what you are telling me. So, may I ask why your employer has sent you here?"

"Mr. Jackson, he has plans for the area you've been working in. And because of your diligence and devotion, his plans include a position for you."

Vicenzi spoke up, "Our employer wants to turn your area into a gardening showcase where you will be head gardener. A place where the people of your complex and others can go and enjoy the outdoors. Where they can learn something about growing plants. He believes it is important to reconnect people with nature. And he thinks you could be a great asset in explaining and showing why that reconnection is important."

"Even so. How will you get all those people to the area safely?"

"The transportation system you use to access the area will be restored for human use. People will ride in comfort to and from the area."

"But one thing we want to emphasize," said Alisi, "the gardening is of primary importance. This will not be an amusement park but a working garden. People will be able to volunteer their time and will be rewarded with the fruits of their labor. Just as you have been," said Alisi, motioning to the tomatoes that Davide had brought home and set on the table.

"And the government is okay with the plans of your employer?" asked Davide with surprise in his voice.

"Mr. Jackson," said Alisi. "The government and other powerful interests I could mention are eager to see that our employer's plans come to fruition. Their only requirement is that all those directing the work be certified."

*The other interests must be the Ems, thought Davide.*

"Well," he said quietly. "You know everything so you know I am not certified."

"But you could become certified. You have more talent than most certified gardeners. And of course, our employer will pick up all costs. The only thing required of you is that you show the same diligence and devotion to learning that you have shown to your garden."

Davide's heart leapt. "I think I can do that."

"Good, we have an understanding then. You will start gardening studies as soon as possible. By the time you are finished the project will be well underway. Thank you and good luck with your studies." The men shook Davide's hand and left.

Davide sat at his kitchen table studying the tomatoes he had brought home with him. He called Sigmund into the room and told him that he was going to be a certified gardener. He was going to make gardening his real vocation. He was astonished at what had just happened. Sigmund only half understood but remarked at what good news it was.

Sigmund began dinner preparations.

Davide sat at the table watching Sigmund. He still couldn't believe it. He forgot the government machinations he had suffered through. He forgot the pain of his losses. He only remembered the smell of tomatoes ripening in the sun and the smile on his grandmother's face.

# ABOUT THE AUTHOR

D.W. Patterson lives in the USA with his beautiful wife Sarah. He studied physics and read classic science fiction in college and then worked for many years as an electronic design engineer.

Now he's trying to write stories like the ones he once loved. See his website: dwpatterson.com for more information.

Hard Science Fiction – Old School.

## Also By This Author:

**The Future Chron Universe:**

To date the Future Chron Universe has:

**51 Amazon Top 100's**

**(15 in the Top 10)**

In chronological order.

Volume numbers indicate Universe order.

Book numbers indicate Series order.

***From The Earth Series***

**(Novellas except where noted):**

**Volume 1, Book 1 – *Whatsoever You Do***

**Volume 2, Book 2 – *War Through The Pines***

**Volume 3, Book 3 – *Vigilance***

**Volume 4, Book 4 – *To Tend And Watch Over***

**Volume 5, Book 5 – *Union***

**Volume 6, Book 6 – *Circle Of Retribution***

**Volume 7, Book 7 – *Freedom From Want***

**Volume 8, Book 8 – *Break Up***

Volume 9, Book 9 – *Kuiper Station*

Volume 10, Book 10 – *The Cloud*

Volume 11, Book 11 – *First Interstellar* – A Short Novel

## *Wormhole Series*

(Novels):

Volume 12, Book 1 – *Mach's Metric*

Volume 13, Book 2 – *Mach's Mission*

## *Open Space Series*

(Short Stories):

Volume 14, Book 1 – *Open Space*

Volume 15, Book 2 – *The Old World*

Volume 16, Book 3 – *Insurrect*

Volume 17, Book 4 – *Second Beam*

Volume 18, Book 5 – *All For One*

Volume 19, Book 6 – *One For All*

Volume 20, Book 7 – *Shotgun*

Volume 21, Book 8 – *Allison*

## *To The Stars Series*

(Novellas):

Volume 22, Book 1 – *First One Hundred*

Volume 23, Book 2 – *First Dark Ages*

Volume 24, Book 3 – *Second One Hundred*

Volume 25, Book 4 – *Second Dark Ages*

Volume 26, Book 5 – *Path Of The Long March*

## *Wormhole Series*

(Novel):

Volume 27, Book 3 – *Mach's Legacy*

## *Robot Series*

(Novels):

Volume 28, Book 1 – *Spin-Two*

Volume 29, Book 2 – *Robot Planet*

Volume 30, Book 3 – *The Lattice Of Space*

## *Time Series*

(Novels):

**Volume 31, Book 1 – *Time Wars***

**Volume 32, Book 2 – *Time's End***

**Volume 33, Book 3 – *Frozen Time***

## The Remembered Earth Universe:

To date the Remembered Earth Universe has:

**8 Amazon Top 100's**

### *Cislunar Series*

**(Short Stories):**

**Volume 1, Book 1 – *US Tugs***

**Volume 2, Book 2 – *Prototype***

**Volume 3, Book 3 – *L1 Or Bust***

**Volume 4, Book 4 – *Guidance Box***

**Volume 5, Book 5 – *Air Brakes***

**Volume 6, Book 6 – *View Point***

**Volume 7, Book 7 – *Space Truck***

**Volume 8, Book 8 – *Dark Side*** – *In Progress*

## The Manifold Earth Universe:

**Volume 1, Book 1 – *The Realm* – *In Progress***

## Don't miss out!

Visit the website below and you can sign up to receive emails whenever D.W. Patterson publishes a new book. There's no charge and no obligation.

https://books2read.com/r/B-A-DPWE-YUFJC

BOOKS 2 READ

Connecting independent readers to independent writers.